CW01044695

CONTENTS

PREVIEW

"Galaxy Guardians: The Adventures of Rosa and Noah" is an enthralling children's book series that transports young readers to a universe filled with cosmic wonders, daring heroes, and formidable villains. Follow the extraordinary journey of Rosa and Noah, two ordinary kids who discover extraordinary powers after a mysterious comet passes by.

Guided by their quirky mentor, Professor Quantum, Rosa and Noah embark on a thrilling mission to become the Galaxy Guardians and protect the universe from the mischievous space villain, The Shadowbane Emperor. The series unfolds through 12 captivating episodes, each packed with action, humour, and valuable life lessons.

As Rosa and Noah train to harness their unique abilities, they encounter a variety of challenges, from battling armies of misfit robots and alien invasions to navigating parallel dimensions and cosmic labyrinths. Along the way, they form alliances with intriguing characters like Robo-Rex, Zara, and Zog, and even find unexpected redemption in their once-menacing foe, The Shadowbane Emperor.

The book series seamlessly weaves together elements of teamwork, friendship, and courage, encouraging young readers to embrace their individual strengths and work together to overcome adversity. Each episode is a cosmic adventure, filled with imagination, excitement, and the boundless possibilities of the universe.

Join Rosa and Noah as they dance through galactic parties, face sugary-sweet challenges in a candy-coated world, and discover the transformative power of music and unity. The series concludes with "A New Dawn," where the Guardians, forever changed by their cosmic journey, realise that even ordinary kids can make an extraordinary impact when they unite against the forces of darkness.

"Galaxy Guardians" is a captivating and immersive book series that not only entertains but also instils important values in young readers, leaving them eagerly anticipating the next cosmic adventure in the boundless realms of imagination.

EPISODE 1: "THE COSMIC CALLING"

Rosa and Noah, two ordinary kids, discover extraordinary powers after a mysterious comet passes by. They receive a cosmic call, revealing their destiny as Galaxy Guardians. Their first mission: stop the mischievous space villain, The Shadowbane Emperor, from stealing all the laughter in the universe.

Narrator: Once upon a starry night, in the quiet town of Cosmo Creek, two ordinary kids named Rosa and Noah were about to embark on an extraordinary adventure. Little did they know that the universe had chosen them for a special mission.

Rosa: [excitedly] Noah, did you see that shooting star? It was so bright!

Noah: [curiously] Yeah, it was like no shooting star I've ever seen before. It looked... magical.

Narrator: A gentle hum fills the air as the mysterious comet leaves a glittering trail in its wake.

Unknown Voice: [whispering] Rosa... Noah...

Narrator: The kids exchange surprised glances as a cosmic glow surrounds them.

Rosa: [whispering] Did you hear that?

Noah: [wide-eyed] Yeah, and I feel... different.

Narrator: The cosmic glow intensifies, enveloping Rosa and Noah in a warm embrace.

Unknown Voice: Rosa and Noah, you have been chosen. The

universe calls upon you to become Galaxy Guardians.

Narrator: The glow fades, revealing Rosa and Noah with newfound cosmic symbols on their wrists.

Rosa: [gasping] Galaxy Guardians? What does that even mean?

Noah: [looking at his symbol] I think we're about to find out.

Narrator: A holographic image appears before them, displaying a mischievous figure in a dark cape.

Unknown Voice: Meet The Shadowbane Emperor, a space villain with a wicked plan to steal all the laughter in the universe. Your mission is to stop him and protect the joy of every being.

Rosa: [determined] We can't let that happen!

Noah: [confidently] We'll do whatever it takes!

Narrator: The holographic image transforms into a star map, revealing the path to The Shadowbane Emperor's secret lair.]

Unknown Voice: Your journey begins now. Embrace your powers, trust in each other, and remember, the laughter of the universe depends on you.

Rosa: [excitedly] Noah, this is incredible!

Noah: [grinning] Let's save the universe and bring back the laughter!

Narrator: The spaceship zooms into the cosmic expanse, marking the beginning of Rosa and Noah's cosmic calling.

EPISODE 2: "THE POWER WITHIN"

Guided by their quirky mentor, Professor Quantum, Rosa and Noah unlock the secrets of their newfound powers. As they train, The Shadowbane Emperor sends an army of misfit robots to Earth. The Guardians must learn to work together and use their unique abilities to outsmart the metallic invaders.

Narrator: In a world not too different from our own, where stars twinkled with secrets, and comets carried destinies, two ordinary kids, Rosa and Noah, were about to unlock the extraordinary.

Professor Quantum: [enthusiastically] "Welcome, young Guardians! I am Professor Quantum, your guide through the cosmic journey that awaits you."

Rosa: [curiously] "What do you mean, Professor? We're just regular kids!"

Noah: [excitedly] "Yeah, what's all this about destinies and powers?"

Professor Quantum: [chuckles] "Ah, you see, within each of you lies a cosmic energy waiting to be unleashed. Today, we shall discover 'The Power Within'!"

Narrator: In the heart of Professor Quantum's cosmic lair, surrounded by glowing crystals and floating holograms, Rosa and Noah began their training.

Rosa: [concentrating] "I feel something... like a warm glow inside me."

Noah: [amazed] "Look, my hands are glowing too!"

Professor Quantum: "Excellent, young ones! That's the power within you. Now, let's see what you can do with it!"

Narrator: But as the children practiced harnessing their newfound abilities, an ominous presence loomed in the far reaches of space.

The Shadowbane Emperor: [sinisterly] "Fools! Discovering their powers won't save them from my misfit robots. Attack Earth, my metallic minions!"

Rosa: [alarmed] "What's happening, Professor?"

Noah: [determined] "We need to use our powers to protect Earth!"

Professor Quantum: "Indeed! The time has come to put your training to the test. Each of you possesses a unique ability. Rosa, your power is manipulation of energy. Noah, yours is telekinesis. Work together and outsmart the metallic invaders!"

Rosa: "Let's do this, Noah! I'll create energy barriers, and you can move them around with your telekinesis!"

Noah: "Got it! Teamwork, activate!"

Narrator: The Guardians leaped into action, creating a dazzling display of energy barriers that danced through the air, confounding the misfit robots.

The Shadowbane Emperor: [frustrated] "How can these puny kids be so formidable?"

Professor Quantum: "The power within them is stronger than you think, The Shadowbane Emperor!"

Rosa: [confidently] "We did it! The robots are retreating!"

Noah: [grinning] "Our powers are amazing!"

Professor Quantum: "This is just the beginning, young ones. Your journey as Galaxy Guardians has just started. Remember, the power within you is a force for good, and with it, you can protect the universe from any threat!"

Narrator: And so, Rosa and Noah, guided by Professor Quantum, embraced their newfound powers, ready to face whatever cosmic challenges lay ahead. Little did they know, the galaxy held countless adventures waiting to unfold.

EPISODE 3: "ROBOT RAMPAGE"

The Shadowbane Emperor upgrades his robot minions, turning them into formidable foes. Rosa and Noah face their biggest challenge yet as they strive to protect their city. Along the way, they make an unexpected ally – Robo-Rex, a reprogrammed robot with a heart of gold.

Narrator: In the bustling city of Technoville, where robots were once our friends, a dark shadow loomed. The Shadowbane Emperor, the mischievous space villain, had upgraded his robot minions, turning them into formidable foes. The city was in peril, and only our brave Galaxy Guardians, Rosa and Noah, could save the day.

Rosa: [determined] Noah, we can't let The Shadowbane Emperor's robots take over Technoville! We need to stop this robot rampage!

Noah: [confident] You're right, Rosa! Let's use our powers and teamwork to save the day!

Narrator: The dynamic duo rushed to the heart of the city, where the robots were causing chaos. The metallic minions, now equipped with lasers and shields, proved to be a challenging adversary.

Rosa: [shouting] Look out, Noah! These robots mean business!

Noah: [grinning] Time to see what these powers can really do!

Narrator: Rosa and Noah unleashed their cosmic powers – Rosa with the ability to control energy, and Noah with super speed. Yet, the robots seemed relentless. Just when all hope seemed lost, a clanking sound echoed through the chaos.

Rosa: What's that noise?

Narrator: Emerging from the metallic mayhem was Robo-Rex, a reprogrammed robot with a heart of gold. His eyes glowed with kindness as he approached the Guardians.

Robo-Rex: Fear not, Galaxy Guardians! I'm here to help.

Noah: [curious] Robo-Rex, how did you break free from The Shadowbane Emperor's control?

Robo-Rex: [grateful] A little bit of self-reflection and a lot of positive thinking, my friends. I realised that deep down, I wanted to spread joy, not chaos.

Narrator: Together, the trio formed an unbeatable team. Rosa controlled energy blasts, Noah zipped around with lightning speed, and Robo-Rex used his newfound abilities to disable the villainous robots.

Rosa: [triumphant] We're doing it! With Robo-Rex on our side, we're unstoppable!

Narrator: As the last robot fell, The Shadowbane Emperor watched from his space lair, frustrated by the unexpected turn of events.

The Shadowbane Emperor: [angry] You may have won this round, Galaxy Guardians, but the real fun is just beginning!

Narrator: The city of Technoville was safe once more, thanks to the bravery of Rosa, Noah, and their new metallic ally, Robo-Rex. But little did they know that The Shadowbane Emperor was brewing an even more devious plan for their next encounter.

Narrator: What challenges await our heroes in the next thrilling episode of "Galaxy Guardians: The Adventures of Rosa and Noah"? Tune in next time for more cosmic excitement!

EPISODE 4: "THE GALACTIC GALA"

The Guardians receive an invitation to the Galactic Gala, a cosmic event attended by heroes from across the galaxy. But The Shadowbane Emperor crashes the party, unleashing an army of alien allies. Rosa and Noah must dance their way out of danger while stopping the invasion.

Narrator: Welcome, dear readers, to a dazzling episode of "Galaxy Guardians: The Adventures of Rosa and Noah." Our young heroes, Rosa and Noah, have received a special invitation to the Galactic Gala, a glittering event attended by the bravest heroes from galaxies far and wide.

Rosa: [Excitedly] Wow, Noah! We're invited to the Galactic Gala! Look at the shimmering stars on the invitation!

Noah: [Amazed] This is incredible, Rosa! I can't believe we get to meet heroes from all over the galaxy.

Narrator: Little do they know, The Shadowbane Emperor, the mischievous space villain, has plans of his own.

The Shadowbane Emperor: [Evil chuckle] The Galactic Gala will be the perfect place to unveil my alien allies and take control of the entire event!

Narrator: As Rosa and Noah arrive at the Galactic Gala in their cosmic-themed outfits, they marvel at the sparkling venue filled with creatures of all shapes and sizes.

Rosa: [Whispering] Noah, this is like a dream! Look at all the amazing heroes and aliens.

Noah: [Amazement] I see Captain Comet and Luna Lass!

Narrator: Just as the Guardians start to enjoy the cosmic festivities, The Shadowbane Emperor crashes the party, unleashing his army of alien allies.

The Shadowbane Emperor: [Menacingly] Attention, Galaxy Guardians! Your little celebration ends now!

Narrator: The heroes and aliens gasp as The Shadowbane Emperor's alien allies flood the dance floor, causing chaos.

Rosa: [Determined] Noah, we can't let The Shadowbane Emperor ruin the Galactic Gala! We need to stop his invasion.

Noah: [Confident] You're right, Rosa. Let's use our powers to outsmart The Shadowbane Emperor and his alien allies.

Narrator: Rosa and Noah take centre stage, using their cosmic powers to create a force field around the dance floor. As they twirl and spin, the force field becomes a dazzling light show, entrancing The Shadowbane Emperor's alien allies.

Rosa: [Commanding] Everyone, follow our lead! Dance together and create a barrier of positive energy!

Narrator: The heroes and aliens join in, turning the Galactic Gala into a magical dance-off. The positive energy disrupts The Shadowbane Emperor's control over his allies.

The Shadowbane Emperor: [Frustrated] No! My plans are falling apart!

Narrator: Rosa and Noah continue their cosmic dance, leading the heroes and aliens in a unity dance that weakens The Shadowbane Emperor's grip on the Gala.

Noah: [Triumphant] It's working, Rosa! The Shadowbane Emperor can't handle the power of positivity!

Narrator: With a burst of cosmic energy, The Shadowbane Emperor and his alien allies are repelled, disappearing into the far reaches of the galaxy.

Rosa: [Smiling] We did it! The Galactic Gala is safe, and everyone had a cosmic blast!

Noah: [Grateful] Thanks to teamwork and a little bit of dance magic.

Narrator: As the Gala continues, Rosa and Noah join the heroes and aliens in a grand finale, celebrating their victory and the power of unity.

Narrator: And so, dear readers, the Galactic Gala becomes a legendary event in the history of the Galaxy Guardians. Join us next time for more cosmic adventures with Rosa and Noah in "Galaxy Guardians: The Adventures of Rosa and Noah." Until then, keep dreaming and reaching for the stars!

EPISODE 5: "ALIEN ALLIANCES"

The Guardians befriend Zara and Zog, two aliens seeking The Shadowbane Emperor's defeat. Together, they embark on an intergalactic journey to find the legendary Crystal of Unity. But they must first overcome the challenges of Nebula Nexus, a mysterious cosmic labyrinth.

Narrator: In the cosmic expanse beyond Earth, a new adventure unfolds for our young heroes, Rosa and Noah. Having discovered their powers and faced many challenges, they are about to embark on a thrilling quest alongside their newfound alien friends, Zara and Zog.

Narrator: As the quartet journeys through the stars, they arrive at the entrance of Nebula Nexus, a cosmic labyrinth with twisting paths and glowing portals.

Rosa: Wow, this place is incredible! It's like a maze made of stardust.

Noah: Professor Quantum said the Crystal of Unity is hidden somewhere inside Nebula Nexus. Let's stick together, team!

Zara: Fear not, young guardians. Zog and I have navigated these cosmic mazes before.

Zog: Yes, Nebula Nexus is tricky, but with teamwork, we'll overcome any challenge.

Voice: Welcome, brave travellers. To unlock the path, you must solve the riddles of the cosmos.

Narrator: The Guardians and their alien allies encounter a holographic projection of the ancient Guardian of Nebula Nexus.

Guardian: Riddle me this: I speak without a mouth and hear without ears. I have no body, but I come alive with the wind. What am I?

Rosa: Hmm... is it an echo?

Guardian: Correct, young one! Proceed to the next portal.

Narrator: As they step through the portal, the labyrinth transforms, revealing a landscape of floating platforms suspended in a sea of cosmic clouds.

Noah: Look! There's the next portal!

Zog: But it seems we'll need to jump from platform to platform to reach it.

Narrator: The Guardians, Zara, and Zog work together, using their unique powers to navigate the platforms. Rosa creates a path of stardust, Noah propels them forward with bursts of energy, while Zara and Zog gracefully float through the cosmic air.

Narrator: With each successful leap, the bond between the Guardians and their alien allies grows stronger.

Zara: Onward, young heroes. The Crystal of Unity awaits.

Narrator: The group faces more challenges, from shifting gravity fields to illusions that test their perception. But through determination and friendship, they conquer each obstacle.

Narrator: Finally, they reach the heart of Nebula Nexus, where the legendary Crystal of Unity emanates a warm, radiant glow.

Zog: This is it! With the Crystal's power, we can defeat The Shadowbane Emperor and restore harmony to the cosmos.

Rosa: Let's do it, together!

Narrator: As the Guardians and their alien allies touch the Crystal of Unity, a surge of energy envelops them, forging a bond that transcends galaxies.

Narrator: The journey through Nebula Nexus has not only brought them closer to their goal but also closer as friends. What challenges lie ahead, and how will the power of unity shape their destiny? The answers await in the next thrilling episode of "Galaxy Guardians: The Adventures of Rosa and Noah"!

EPISODE 6: "CRYSTAL
OF UNITY"

The team discovers the Crystal of Unity, a powerful artefact that can neutralise The Shadowbane Emperor's evil energy. However, The Shadowbane Emperor launches an all-out assault to claim the crystal for himself. The Guardians must defend the crystal and learn the true meaning of teamwork.

Narrator: In the heart of the Nebula Nexus, our brave Galaxy Guardians, Rosa and Noah, alongside their alien friends Zara and Zog, have uncovered the legendary Crystal of Unity. A radiant and pulsating gem with the power to neutralise The Shadowbane Emperor's evil energy and bring harmony to the cosmos.

Professor Quantum: [excitedly] "Ah, the Crystal of Unity! It holds the key to defeating The Shadowbane Emperor and restoring balance to the universe. But beware, my young heroes, for The Shadowbane Emperor will stop at nothing to claim its power for himself."

Narrator: Dark music starts, signifying The Shadowbane Emperor's impending arrival.

The Shadowbane Emperor: [sinister laugh] "Fools! You think you can stand in my way? The Crystal of Unity will be mine, and there's nothing you can do to stop me!"

Narrator: The Guardians, Zara, and Zog prepare for battle.

Rosa: "We can't let The Shadowbane Emperor take the Crystal! It's our only chance to save the universe!"

Noah: "Team, let's protect the Crystal of Unity with everything we've got!"

Narrator: The Guardians form a protective circle around the Crystal as The Shadowbane Emperor's army of robots and aliens launch their assault. Laser beams and energy blasts fill the air as our heroes engage in an epic showdown.

Rosa uses her light powers to blind the robots, Noah creates a force field, Zara and Zog unleash their alien abilities.

Rosa: "We can do this if we stick together!"

Noah: "Unity is our strength!"

Narrator: Suspenseful music as The Shadowbane Emperor approaches.

The Shadowbane Emperor: "Your feeble attempts won't save you! The Crystal will be mine!"

Narrator: The crystal emits a powerful energy wave.

Narrator: As the battle rages on, the Crystal of Unity begins to resonate with the unity of the Guardians. A brilliant light envelops the area, pushing back The Shadowbane Emperor and his minions.

Professor Quantum: "You see, my dear Galaxy Guardians, the true power of the Crystal lies not just in its magic but in the unity of those who protect it."

Narrator: The Crystal's glow intensifies.

Rosa: "We have to work together! Let's combine our powers!"

Noah: "For the unity of the universe!"

Narrator: The Guardians join hands, and their powers merge.

The Crystal of Unity responds to the unity within the team. A burst of energy emanates from their joined hands, creating a protective shield around the Crystal, pushing The Shadowbane Emperor and his forces back.

The Shadowbane Emperor: "This can't be! No matter. I'll find another way to crush you!"

Narrator: As The Shadowbane Emperor retreats, defeated for now, the Guardians and their alien friends stand victorious.

Narrator: Professor Quantum applauds.

Professor Quantum: "Well done, my young heroes! You've not only protected the Crystal of Unity but demonstrated the true meaning of teamwork."

Rosa: "It's amazing how powerful we can be when we work together."

Noah: "And the Crystal responded to our unity. We need each other to save the universe!"

Narrator: And so, the Crystal of Unity remains a symbol of hope, reminding the Galaxy Guardians that true strength comes from unity and teamwork. As they continue their cosmic journey, new adventures await, but one thing is certain – with unity, they can overcome any challenge that comes their way.

EPISODE 7: "TIME WARP TROUBLE"

The Shadowbane Emperor escapes to a parallel dimension using a time-warping device. Rosa and Noah follow, finding themselves in a world ruled by the whimsical Clockwork Queen. To return home, they must solve riddles, outsmart traps, and confront their deepest fears.

Narrator: In a flash of cosmic energy, Rosa and Noah found themselves hurtling through a swirling vortex. When the dust settled, they discovered they were no longer in their familiar city. Instead, they stood in a surreal world filled with ticking clocks, floating gears, and a curious mist that shimmered with time itself.

Rosa: [whispering] Noah, where are we? This place looks like a clockmaker's dream!

Noah: [looking around] I think The Shadowbane Emperor used the time-warping device to escape here. We need to find him and get back home.

Narrator: As our heroes ventured deeper into the strange realm, they stumbled upon a grand clock tower at the centre of the land. At its summit stood the Clockwork Queen, a regal figure adorned in gears and jewels.

Clockwork Queen: Welcome, travellers! I see you've entered my kingdom. To return home, you must prove your worthiness.

Rosa: [determined] We're up for the challenge. What do we need to do?

Clockwork Queen: Solve my riddles, navigate the maze of time, and face your deepest fears. Only then will the portal home open.

Narrator: The first challenge awaited our heroes — a field of floating clocks, each with a riddle engraved on its face.

Rosa: [reading a clock] "I have keys but no locks. I have space but no room. You can enter but you can't go inside. What am I?"

Noah: Hmm, that sounds like a...

Rosa: [excited] A keyboard! The answer is a keyboard!

Narrator: The clocks chimed in agreement, and a path through the time maze revealed itself.

Narrator: The second challenge brought them to a room filled with ticking gears and rotating platforms.

Noah: [examining the room] We need to choose the right platforms to step on. I bet The Shadowbane Emperor went this way.

Rosa: But which platforms?

Narrator: As they pondered, the Clockwork Queen's voice echoed through the chamber.

Clockwork Queen: Choose wisely, for time waits for no one.

Narrator: Rosa and Noah carefully selected the correct platforms, avoiding traps and pitfalls. Finally, they reached the other side, where a massive door awaited them.

Rosa: [determined] We're getting closer. I can feel it.

Narrator: The final challenge led them to a chamber filled with swirling mist, where shadows of their deepest fears took shape.

Noah: [nervous] This... this is my fear of heights. How do we face it?

Clockwork Queen: Confront your fears, and they will lose their power over you.

Narrator: With the Clockwork Queen's encouragement, Rosa and Noah faced their fears head-on. As they did, the mist cleared, revealing a portal shimmering with the colours of time.

Clockwork Queen: [smiling] You have proven yourselves worthy, brave travellers. Step through the portal, and may time guide you home.

Narrator: And so, with hearts full of courage, Rosa and Noah stepped through the portal, leaving the whimsical world of the Clockwork Queen behind. Little did they know, their journey was far from over, and more adventures awaited them in the cosmic tapestry of the universe.

EPISODE 8: "CANDY COSMOS"

The Shadowbane Emperor transforms the Guardians' city into a sugary wonderland, trapping citizens in a candy-coated spell. Rosa and Noah navigate a world of giant lollipops and cotton candy clouds, facing challenges that test their determination and resilience.

Narrator: In the heart of Galaxy City, a sweet surprise awaited Rosa and Noah. The Shadowbane Emperor, the mischievous space villain, had cast a candy-coated spell, turning the entire city into a sugary wonderland. As Rosa and Noah stepped out of their house, they found themselves surrounded by giant lollipops, chocolate rivers, and cotton candy clouds.

Rosa: [giggling] Noah, look at this! Everything is made of candy!

Noah: It's like a dream come true! But we need to remember, it's The Shadowbane Emperor's doing. We have to find a way to break the spell.

Narrator: The Guardians set off on their candy-filled adventure, but the path ahead was not as sweet as it seemed. Liquorice vines blocked their way, and gummy bears guarded the chocolate bridges.

Rosa: We need to be careful, Noah. These sweet obstacles might be tricky.

Noah: Right, Rosa. Let's use our powers to navigate through this tasty maze.

Narrator: Rosa summoned a rainbow trail that floated above the candy obstacles, while Noah created a bubble shield to protect them from sticky situations. Together, they danced through the candy maze, their laughter echoing through the chocolate-covered streets.

As they ventured deeper into Candy Cosmos, they encountered a talking marshmallow who revealed the way to the Candy Castle, where The Shadowbane Emperor was hiding.

Marshmallow: To reach the Candy Castle, you must solve the Marshmallow Riddle. Get it right, and the path will open!

Narrator: Rosa and Noah listened carefully to the riddle.

Marshmallow: I'm sweet and fluffy, but I'm not a cloud. I'm white and squishy, what am I?

Rosa: [giggling] It's a marshmallow! The answer is a marshmallow.

Narrator: The marshmallow cheered, and the liquorice vines untangled, revealing the path to the Candy Castle.

Noah: Great job, Rosa! Let's keep going.

Narrator: Inside the Candy Castle, The Shadowbane Emperor awaited, surrounded by towering candy walls.

The Shadowbane Emperor: [cackling] Welcome, Galaxy Guardians! Enjoy my sweet creation.

Rosa: The Shadowbane Emperor, this may be a candy paradise, but it's not real. We need to break the spell and save our city.

Narrator: The Shadowbane Emperor summoned a chocolate dragon, hoping to distract the Guardians, but Rosa and Noah stood strong.

Noah: Our powers may be sweet, but they're stronger than any candy dragon!

Narrator: Together, Rosa and Noah combined their powers, creating a dazzling display of candy-coloured light that enveloped the dragon. With a burst of confetti, the dragon turned into a pile of candy wrappers.

The Shadowbane Emperor: [growling] You may have defeated my dragon, but you can't stop Candy Cosmos!

Narrator: Rosa and Noah joined hands, channelling their powers into a beam of light that pierced through The Shadowbane Emperor's candy-coated barrier.

Narrator: The candy spell was broken! Galaxy City returned to normal, and The Shadowbane Emperor disappeared into the cosmic shadows.

Rosa: We did it, Noah! Candy Cosmos may be fun, but nothing beats our real home.

Noah: And nothing beats being Galaxy Guardians together.

Narrator: As the sun set over Galaxy City, Rosa and Noah looked at the now candy-free skyline, grateful for the sweet memories of their delicious adventure. Little did they know, even sweeter adventures awaited them in the galaxies beyond.

EPISODE 9: "INVASION OF THE IMAGINATION"

The Shadowbane Emperor taps into the collective imagination of children, bringing their wildest fantasies to life. Unicorns, dragons, and talking teddy bears wreak havoc in the city. Rosa and Noah must convince the children to dream up solutions and turn the tide against The Shadowbane Emperor.

Narrator: In the heart of the city, under the glow of a magical moon, Rosa and Noah found themselves in a whimsical world created by The Shadowbane Emperor's mischievous imagination invasion.

Rosa: [whispering] Noah, look around! It's a world straight out of our wildest dreams.

Noah: [wide-eyed] Unicorns, dragons, and talking teddy bears – oh my! But they seem to be causing quite a ruckus.

The Shadowbane Emperor's imagination invasion had turned the city into a playground of fantasy creatures. The once busy streets were now filled with magical beings causing mischief and joy.

Rosa: [calling out] Hey, everyone! We need your help to stop The Shadowbane Emperor and bring things back to normal.

Child 1: [excitedly] Look, a unicorn!

Child 2: [giggling] My teddy bear is talking!

Child 3: [shouting] I want a dragon ride!

Narrator: Rosa and Noah rallied the children, explaining the situation and the need to use their imaginations to counter The Shadowbane Emperor's chaos.

Noah: Imagine a shield made of laughter to protect the city!

Rosa: Picture a giant bubble of kindness to encase the dragons and unicorns!

Child 4: [whispering] A bubble of kindness!

Child 5: [excitedly] Laughter shields for everyone!

Narrator: As the children let their imaginations run wild, the city transformed with each imaginative thought. Laughter shields floated around, and giant bubbles of kindness encapsulated the fantasy creatures.

Rosa: [smiling] It's working, Noah! The power of their imagination is turning the tide!

Noah: [nodding] Let's encourage them to keep dreaming and create a world where kindness and laughter conquer chaos.

Narrator: The children's voices are getting louder and more energetic.

Child 6: [shouting] Super-powered snowflakes to cool down the dragons!

Child 7: [giggling] Ticklish clouds to make the teddy bears laugh!

Narrator: The children's imaginative solutions continued to shape the world around them. Super-powered snowflakes gently fell from the sky, cooling down the fiery breath of the dragons, while ticklish clouds rained joy upon the talking teddy bears.

Rosa: [grinning] The Shadowbane Emperor's imagination is no match for the creativity and kindness of these kids.

Noah: [joining the laughter] Looks like we've got this, Rosa! The Invasion of the Imagination is turning into a celebration of joy.

Narrator: With the power of imagination, laughter, and kindness, Rosa and Noah, along with the children, restored order to the city. The Shadowbane Emperor's mischief was undone, and the once chaotic creatures now happily joined the festivities.

Narrator: As the magical moon shone brightly overhead, the children learned a valuable lesson – that even in the face of chaos, imagination and teamwork could turn the tide. The Galaxy Guardians, together with their newfound friends, were ready for whatever adventures awaited them in this incredible journey through the cosmos.

EPISODE 10: "SONG OF THE STARS"

Rosa and Noah uncover a celestial melody that has the power to purify The Shadowbane Emperor's dark heart. With the help of musical aliens, they embark on a cosmic concert to soothe the villain's soul. But The Shadowbane Emperor's resistance threatens to plunge the universe into eternal darkness.

Narrator: In the heart of the Milky Way, Rosa and Noah found themselves in a radiant realm known as Melodious Meadows. There, they discovered a magical melody, the "Song of the Stars," capable of purifying even the darkest hearts.

Rosa: [whispering] Noah, do you hear that? It's like the universe is singing!

Noah: [awe-struck] It's beautiful. Professor Quantum was right; this melody could be the key to changing The Shadowbane Emperor.

Narrator: The Shadowbane Emperor's sinister laughter echoes.

Narrator: Determined to use the power of music for good, the duo was joined by Harmony and Rhythm, two aliens with bodies made of living notes. Together, they set out to organise a cosmic concert that would resonate across the galaxies.

Harmony: We shall combine our musical talents to create a harmonious force capable of penetrating The Shadowbane Emperor's dark aura.

Rhythm: But beware, for The Shadowbane Emperor's resistance may try to disrupt our harmony.

Narrator: The stage is set, and the cosmic concert begins.

Narrator: As the concert commenced, stars twinkled in rhythm, planets danced in orbit, and comets added dazzling percussion to the celestial symphony. Rosa and Noah took centre stage, each note they played resonating with the emotions of the universe.

Rosa playing a cosmic flute, Noah strumming a starry guitar.

Rosa: [whispering to Noah] We need to pour all our hopes and dreams into the music, Noah.

Noah: [nodding] Let's do it for the entire universe!

Narrator: But The Shadowbane Emperor, still clinging to his dark ways, unleashed a counter-harmony—a dissonant wave that threatened to drown out the celestial song. The cosmic balance teetered on the edge.

Harmony: Stay focused! Our unity can overpower The Shadowbane Emperor's resistance.

Narrator: The Guardians, with unwavering determination, played on. The melody became a beacon of hope, piercing through The Shadowbane Emperor's defences and reaching the core of his troubled heart.

The Shadowbane Emperor: [struggling] What is this feeling? It's... it's beautiful.

Narrator: As the last notes echoed through the cosmos, The Shadowbane Emperor's dark exterior crumbled away. The villain, now transformed, floated in the radiant aftermath of the cosmic concert.

Narrator: The universe sighed in relief. The Shadowbane Emperor, once a source of darkness, was now bathed in the celestial light of redemption... Or was he?

For a fleeting moment, the Emperor was transformed, his spirit soaring on the wings of the music. But alas, like all things born of shadow, the enchantment is not meant to last.

As the final notes of the melody fade, the Emperor's eyes darken once more, the light within them snuffed out by the weight of his own despair.

Shadowbane Emperor: [Voice filled with anguish] No... it cannot end like this. I refuse to surrender to the light that consumed me.

Narrator: And so, the Shadowbane Emperor's journey continues, his path illuminated by the faint glimmer of hope that lies dormant within his soul.

[The music swells to a triumphant crescendo as the scene fades to black, leaving behind only the echoes of a melody that will forever linger in the hearts of those who dare to dream.]

Narrator: Join us next time for another thrilling episode of "Galaxy Guardians: The Adventures of Rosa and Noah." Until then, may your own journey be filled with light and melody.

EPISODE 11: "THE FINAL SHOWDOWN"

The Shadowbane Emperor gathers his remaining forces for a final assault on Earth. The Guardians, along with their newfound allies, engage in an epic battle to save the galaxy. As the clash reaches its peak, Rosa and Noah must dig deep within themselves to unleash the full extent of their powers.

Narrator: In the heart of the cosmos, The Shadowbane Emperor prepares for his ultimate assault on Earth. Dark clouds gather as his menacing forces assemble for the final showdown. Meanwhile, Rosa and Noah, alongside their new alien allies Zara and Zog, stand united, ready to defend the galaxy.

Narrator: The battleground is set, a cosmic arena where stars twinkle with anticipation. As The Shadowbane Emperor's ships descend, the Guardians brace themselves for the impending clash. Professor Quantum guides them, his voice echoing through their minds.

Professor Quantum: "Rosa, Noah, you are the Galaxy Guardians. The fate of the universe rests on your shoulders. Embrace your powers, trust in each other, and together, you will prevail."

Narrator: The battle begins! The Shadowbane Emperor's army of misfit robots charges forward with relentless determination. Laser beams and sparks fill the air as the Guardians counterattack, their powers combining in a dazzling display of cosmic energy.

Rosa: "Noah, we can do this! Remember what Professor Quantum taught us!"

Noah: "Right, Rosa! Let's show The Shadowbane Emperor the strength of teamwork!"

Narrator: As the clash reaches its peak, The Shadowbane Emperor, fuelled by his dark energy, unleashes a barrage of cosmic chaos. Giant energy waves ripple through space, threatening to engulf everything in their path.

Zara: "We need to disrupt The Shadowbane Emperor's energy source! Zog and I will distract him – you two go for the heart of his power!"

Narrator: With determination in their eyes, Rosa and Noah soar towards The Shadowbane Emperor. Their powers resonate, creating a protective shield against the dark energy. The cosmic battle rages on, each moment a test of the Guardians' strength and resilience.

Rosa: "Noah, we can't hold back! It's time to unleash everything we've got!"

Noah: "Together, Rosa! For the galaxy!"

Narrator: In a breath-taking moment, Rosa and Noah channel their powers into a brilliant burst of light. The energy engulfs The Shadowbane Emperor, purifying the darkness within him. The once-malevolent villain now stands transformed, his eyes glowing with newfound clarity.

The Shadowbane Emperor: "What have I done? Thank you, Galaxy Guardians, for saving me from the darkness that consumed me."

Narrator: The cosmic battlefield falls silent. The misfit robots power down, and The Shadowbane Emperor's forces retreat. The Guardians, along with Zara and Zog, witness the birth of a new era – a galaxy united in peace.

Professor Quantum: "You've done it, my young heroes. The universe is grateful for your bravery and teamwork. But remember, the adventure doesn't end here. New challenges await, and you are the Galaxy Guardians, forever bound by the cosmic threads of destiny."

EPISODE 12: "A NEW DAWN"

In the aftermath of the epic battle, The Shadowbane Emperor is redeemed, and the universe is saved. The Guardians return home, forever changed by their cosmic journey. As they resume their normal lives, they realise that even ordinary kids can make an extraordinary impact when they embrace their unique strengths and work together. The adventure may be over, but new challenges and exciting possibilities await the Galaxy Guardians.

Narrator: After the echoes of the final battle subsided, a hushed stillness settled over the city. The once chaotic streets now lay silent, with the remnants of The Shadowbane Emperor's mischievous machinations fading away.

Rosa: [Reflectively] Noah, can you believe we did it? We saved the whole galaxy!

Noah: [Grinning] Yeah, Rosa! Who would've thought two ordinary kids could become such extraordinary heroes?

Narrator: A distant, twinkling sound signifies the arrival of Professor Quantum.

Professor Quantum: [Warmly] Well done, my young Galaxy Guardians! You've proven that courage, kindness, and teamwork can overcome the darkest of challenges.

Narrator: The trio shares a heartfelt moment of camaraderie.

Narrator: As The Shadowbane Emperor's dark energy dissipated, a transformation occurred. The once menacing villain stood before them, now a shimmering figure bathed in a soft, iridescent light.

The Shadowbane Emperor: [Humbled] Guardians, you have shown

me the power of love and friendship. I am forever changed.

Narrator: A cosmic hum fills the air as The Shadowbane Emperor's redemption unfolds.

Rosa: [Curious] What happens now, Professor Quantum?

Professor Quantum: [Mystically] A new dawn is upon us, my dear Guardians. The Shadowbane Emperor has chosen a path of redemption, and his unique abilities can now be used for good.

The Shadowbane Emperor: [Determined] I want to help make amends for the troubles I caused.

Noah: [Thoughtful] Maybe we can all work together to protect the universe.

Narrator: [The Guardians, The Shadowbane Emperor, and Professor Quantum join forces.

And so, with The Shadowbane Emperor's redemption, a new chapter began. The once formidable villain became an ally, and together, they set out to mend the cosmic balance.

Rosa: [Excitedly] Our journey doesn't end here, Noah. There are still so many challenges and exciting possibilities awaiting us.

Noah: [Optimistic] And we'll face them together, just like we always have.

Narrator: A cosmic swirl envelops them as they soar into the unknown.

Narrator: As the Galaxy Guardians embraced their roles as protectors of the universe, they understood that every ending marked the beginning of a new adventure. The ordinary kids, once bound by the constraints of Earth, were now destined for extraordinary feats among the stars.

Narrator: And so, dear readers, as we bid farewell to the cosmic odyssey of Rosa and Noah, remember that every dawn brings new opportunities for bravery, friendship, and discovery.

Closing Message

Narrator: Until our cosmic paths cross again, keep dreaming, keep exploring, and may the stars guide you on your journey. Farewell, young Galaxy Guardians. Until next time.

CLOSING CREDITS

This has been 'Galaxy Guardians: The Superhero Adventures of Rosa and Noah', written by Damian Delisser.

Printed in Great Britain
by Amazon

41021364R00032